For Jamie and Fiona's gorgeous twins, Poppy and Harryo
R. CURTIS

For my family and Father Christmas xx
R. COBB

PUFFIN BOOKS
Published by the Penguin Group: London, New York,
Australia, Canada, India, Ireland, New Zealand and South Africa
Penguin Books Ltd, Registered Offices: 80 Strand, London WC2R 0RL, England
puffinbooks.com
First published 2012
001 – 10 9 8 7 6 5 4 3 2 1
Text copyright © Richard Curtis, 2012
Illustrations copyright © Rebecca Cobb, 2012
All rights reserved
The moral right of the author and illustrator has been asserted
Made and printed in China
Hardback: 978–0–141–33624–4
Paperback: 978–0–141–33625–1

The EMPTY Stocking

RICHARD CURTIS

With illustrations by Rebecca Cobb

PUFFIN

IT was Christmas night and Mr and Mrs Weston were excited.

As were their twins, **Sam** and **Charlie**.
Who were, despite their names, both girls.

Sam was *Samantha* and Charlie was *Charlotte*, but they were never
called those names – they were always called Sam and Charlie.
They were also, always, twins – both having been born
                    on June the 21st,
                         Midsummer's Day,
                    seven years
                         before.

But their birthday was not the only thing about them that was
the same. They also looked *exactly* the same – although of course
people who really loved them could completely see the difference.

Sam ALWAYS wore her hair in pretty **plaits** –
and Charlie had a little **scar**
on her cheek in the
shape of a fork.

But actually, as children, they couldn't be more **different**.
And on Christmas night that was a serious worry – because
Sam was always *very* well behaved and Charlie was, well, not to
mince words, because this is basically what this story is about –

Charlie was *quite* bad.

Not *really* bad, but, you know, *very* naughty.
Not interested in being obedient. Quite often very grumpy.
Not very fond of telling the complete truth.
But *very* fond of eating sweets,
     making a filthy racket
and having too much
     FUN.

Her parents of course *still* loved
her to bits, loved her as much as Sam,
because that's what parents do.

But, for instance, her teachers found her *very* annoying –
because she was **particularly** naughty at school.

And her next-door neighbours hated her –
because she was *very* naughty at home.

And shopkeepers didn't like her one bit –
because she ate A LOT of their sweets
and *very rarely*
paid for
them.

Anyway – it was Christmas night and as usual
the family watched *Elf*, which was just great. Then Dad read
them *The Night Before Christmas*, which was very good,
and *How the Grinch Stole Christmas*, which was even better.

Then Mum sat at the piano and made them all sing "Santa Claus
is Coming to Town" and, as always, when they got to the bit
about Santa knowing whether you'd been good or bad,
everybody couldn't help looking for
just a moment
in **Charlie's**
direction.

Because this **was** a worry.
There was no way Santa *wouldn't* know
what Charlie had been up to
this year.

But, as usual, when it got late, the children put out their stockings at the end of their beds and left a mince pie, a tangerine and a glass of port for Santa by the chimney. And then headed off, *very* excited, to bed.

And Charlie said to her dad, "Daddy, do you think Santa will bring me anything this year?" And her dad said, "Yes, of course he will, my darling." But, there's no denying it, he was a little bit worried, because this *really* had been Charlie's **naughtiest** year yet. What with the eating-a-**whole**-box-of-chocolates incident.

And the glue-in-the-DVD episode.

And the ice-down-the-back-of-the-teacher's-dress moment.

And the WORSE things.

Then Mum and Dad went upstairs to bed pretty early too, because they'd heard a story about a mum and dad who had stayed up late and *actually* bumped into Santa Claus on the stairs – and Santa Claus had scarpered and they'd had to quickly fill stockings for their kids **themselves** to make up for Santa's hasty exit.

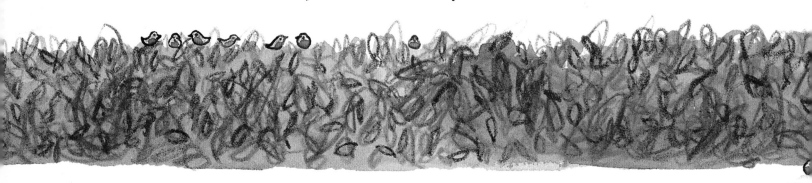

So at ten past eleven they got into their pyjamas,
turned off their lights and, even though they whispered till

midnight, at least they knew that Santa could get on with his job *undisturbed*.

And, of course, that's exactly what Santa did.
At about 1.15 in the morning he arrived in England from Spain
in a *very* good mood, because he was getting quite near home.

He moved up swiftly from Kent,

rushed through London

and sped on to Suffolk,

where **good** Sam

and *naughty* Charlie lived.

He landed in the garden, placed the hungry reindeer near a tasty hedge
(by the way, look out for that next year – if you've got a garden, you'll normally find
that a bit of it has been *mightily munched* on Christmas morning)

and then headed d o w n
the chimney
into the
living room.

Dusting himself off, he crept past Mum and Dad's door
and into the room where the **twins** slept.

And there
he filled
one stocking . . .

And
left
the
other
one
completely
EMPTY.

Because Charlie had indeed been *very* bad that year.

He *never* liked doing it. But, *sometimes*, Santa has to get **tough**.
And this year, in Charlie and Sam's room,
was one of the
get tough times.

He then left their room quickly, drank a bit of port, gobbled the whole tangerine *and* the pie, swooshed up the chimney and headed on.

And left the house *totally* still.

Mum and Dad had no idea of the **terrible thing** that had just happened. Neither did Sam or Charlie. One stocking hung light and empty, and the other swung with the weight of all the wonderful presents.

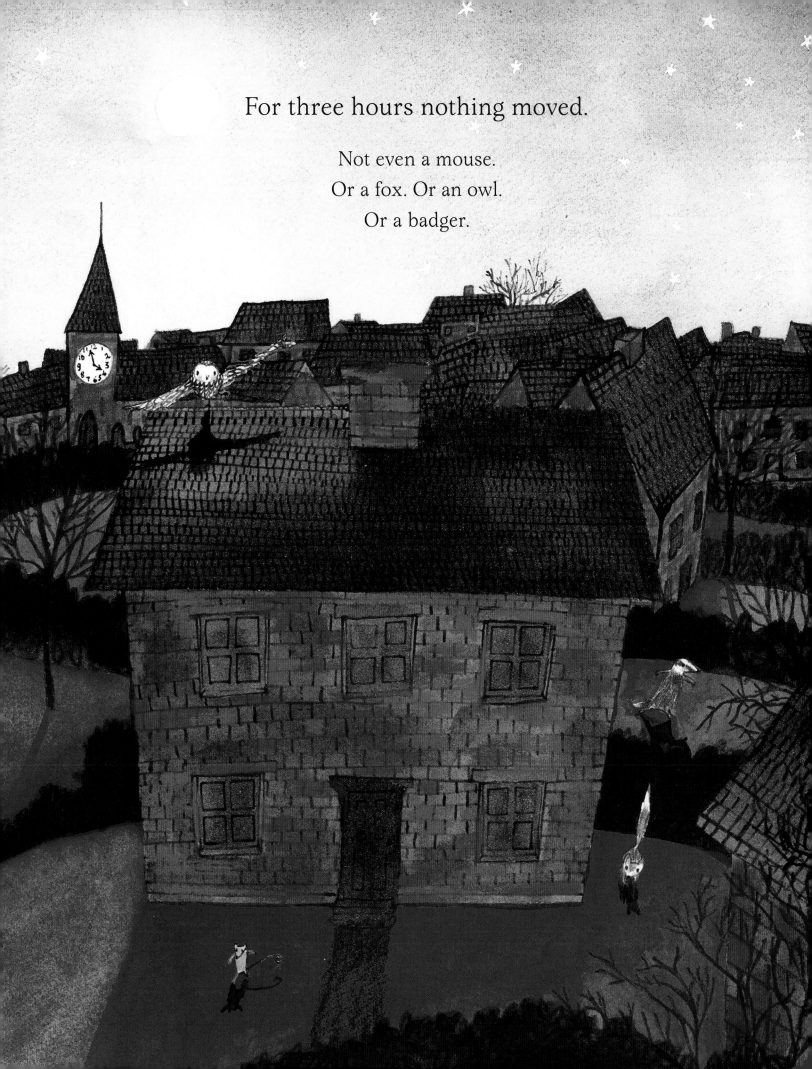

For three hours nothing moved.

Not even a mouse.
Or a fox. Or an owl.
Or a badger.

And then, just by chance, as fate would have it,
at four in the morning, *naughty* Charlie woke up.

And looked down at the end of the bed.

And saw . . .

a
gorgeous,
full
stocking.

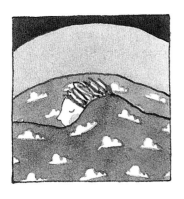

Because, you see, Santa hadn't looked very carefully. And, when Charlie and Sam were sleeping, you couldn't see Sam's plaits and you couldn't see the scar on Charlie's cheek. So they looked *exactly* and *completely* and **utterly the same** . . .

With **disastrous** results.

Charlie was *thrilled* about the stocking and, because she was quite naughty, she decided that she would go and sneak a peek at all her presents before everyone else woke up.

But as she went
    down the bed . . .

she looked across
    at her sister's bed
    and saw . . .

The
EMPTY
stocking.

And she stopped dead.
And she just sat there.
And thought very hard.
With a big frown.

Because no-one had ever really
bothered to notice, but amongst all her
naughtiness Charlie *really* loved her sister.

And sometimes the actual reason she was naughty
was because she **loved** making Sam happy.

And sometimes when she was *really* naughty
it was because she loved making Sam laugh.

And sometimes when she was *really*,
REALLY naughty it was because other
people had been picking on Sam –
and Charlie was
certainly **not**
having that.

And then Charlie thought
about her sweet sister's face in the morning,
when she'd reach for her stocking all *excited* about
the toys and sweets and games she'd find inside . . .

and she would find *nothing* in it at all.

She thought about how Sam would try to be brave,
and how Sam's chin would start to wobble. And she thought
about how she felt whenever Sam was sad – not sad because
Charlie had just sat on her, but really *properly, in-her-heart* sad.

And then, very, very, *very* quietly, so she didn't wake up Sam . . .
naughty Charlie started to move presents from her **full** stocking into
Sam's **empty** one.

Present by present.
One after
the other.

In a totally
mathematical
manner.

Even if she
really liked
something.

Until both stockings were half full.
With *exactly* the same number of
presents. Because **half** was a lot
better than nothing.

And, when she'd made completely sure each stocking was the same,
Charlie breathed a sigh of relief and went back up her bed and back to sleep.

And everything went quiet again. At home.
But not, as it turns out, on Santa's sleigh. Because Santa
was getting near the North Pole when **suddenly** something
very *unexpected* happened.

A light started to FLASH on his Good**Bad**O*Meter*,
the machine that told him which children had been
good and which ones had been **bad**.

And Santa looked *very* suprised indeed,
because this had **never** happened before.

There'd been a last-minute change.

Forty-five minutes later, a very exhausted fat old man with a beard landed on a lawn in Suffolk with a very munched hedge.

And a minute later he was on the stairs **again**, creeping towards the twins' room.

And when he popped his head into the room he saw the two half-filled stockings. And he *smiled*.

And then swiftly, because it was getting very close to the time that children start to wake up, he filled up **both** stockings
> to the **brim**
> > and crept
> > > back down
> > > > the stairs.

But just as he put his head in the chimney
> he had **one** last thought and headed back up the stairs

one last time, and popped **one** last little thing into Charlie's stocking.

Five minutes later Santa flew away in the highest of spirits –
and indeed, just like he used to in the old days,
he hollered for all to hear . . .

Happy Christmas to all

and to all a Good Night!

... Good Night !

Which actually woke up **good** Sam, who looked down her bed and saw
a *completely* **full** stocking, just as she expected. Then she looked across
at *naughty* Charlie's bed, a little bit worried, but she saw, *thank heavens*,
that her sister's stocking was

completely

full

as well.

So she woke Charlie who, for some reason Sam could never explain, looked *very* shocked indeed by their two **full** stockings.

"I suppose," Sam said to her mum later, "it must be because Charlie didn't expect to get any presents *at all* this year."

Then Sam and Charlie both rushed into Mum and Dad's room
and opened *all* their presents,
one
after
another.

And everyone was very happy indeed.

But when the stockings were *completely* empty Charlie happened to put her hand in *just* one more time, *just* to check.

And she was surprised to find a small, bright badge that looked a bit like Rudolph's nose.

She never showed it to anyone,
because she was a bit
embarrassed about it.

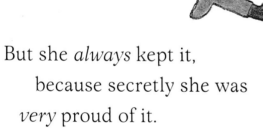

But she *always* kept it,
because secretly she was
very proud of it.

And secretly, although she knew she
was sometimes very naughty indeed,
she also thought it **might** be true . . .

It

just

said

two

words . . .